PETECTIVES

ROBERT J. SMITH

First Rose-Grey Books edition 2013

"The cat is the only animal which accepts the comforts but rejects the bondage of domesticity." - Georges Louis Leclerc de Buffon

CHAPTER 1

It was a clear October night with a big yellow moon hanging in the black sky above me. I was running through the Forest Heights subdivision as fast as four paws could carry me. I had an appointment with a client and I was already late.

"Yo, Gatsby!" a rough voice barked out. "Get over here! I need to talk to you!" To a human ear that would've just sounded like some mean half-crazed bulldog barking at the moon. To me it was a mean, half-crazed bulldog calling me over to make me even later for my appointment. I decided to go over and see what he

1

wanted; there was a chance that it would be worth my while. I trotted over to his backyard. His name was Percy; his fur was a deep, dark brown and he always had an expression as if he'd spent the day guzzling spoilt milk.

"Get your orange butt over here!" he yelled as he saw me approaching. Before I answered him, I made sure that he was chained to his house. The chain was slack but I could tell how far he could get before his teeth could reach me. I stopped about five feet from where I figured the chain would stop him if he wanted to rip me to cat shreds.

I gave him a big smile. "What do you want, Percival?"

"Why don't you come a little closer?"

"Your breath's strong enough from here. You've got to stop drinking out of the toilet. Or at least wait until somebody flushes." Of course if he was loose, I wouldn't have said that. I'd probably have run to Cuba by now.

"You're pretty funny," he growled. "Look, I've got a message for your boss"

"He's not my boss." I responded. "We're partners!"

"Yeah, whatever. You tell Yoshi that I've got a business opportunity to discuss with him."

"That's out. You know darn well that Yoshi is the ultimate indoor cat. You tell me about this opportunity, then I'll tell him and we'll let you know later. That's how it works."

"Whatever. I ain't dealing with errand boys. I can get you boys ten years worth of catnip – Don't screw it up."

I started to walk away. "OK" I called back, "I'll tell him and maybe we'll get back to you. But if I was you, I wouldn't hold your breath. Well, not without gloves and a hazardous waste suit."

His response was insane barking that rang out through the neighborhood, probably waking up all of the humans in the surrounding houses.

My appointment was in front of the white two-story house on the corner with the huge pine tree that seemed to stretch up to the moon. I was hoping that this would lead to an interesting job. I'd been very idle for the last month and the only other jobs we'd been offered this week was either investigating who had knocked over Mr. Bascom's barbeque, leaving a mess of ashes and used charcoal briquettes in his backyard or finding out who had busted into the Rogers family's garage and raided their freezer. Both of those potential cases seemed so boring that staying home and watching Animal Planet seemed like a more productive use of my time.

As I approached the corner, I got at a good look at the cat that I was supposed to meet as she sat there waiting for me. It may have been the full moon shining down on her or it may have been my imagination but she looked better than a big hunk of fish smothered in tartar sauce sitting in a bowl of buttermilk. She was a white cat with black ears and black patches all over including one around her right eye which was especially cute. She was bigger than me, but this much beauty in a bigger serving was not a bad thing. Whatever this cat needed, I was going to get it for her and then she would marry me out of gratitude and we would have lots of good looking kittens.

"Are you Gatsby?" she asked, breaking me out of my daydream.

"That's me. And would you be the lady in need of my services?" After I had said that I thought that I should probably be more specific. "As a detective? Or a bodyguard?"

When I said "bodyguard" she laughed. Even her mocking laughter was musical. I assumed that she didn't think that a small statured cat would make a good bodyguard. After she got to know me better, she's see how wrong she was.

"I'm sorry," She said, probably after seeing the expression on my face. "I'm sure that you're a great bodyguard but it's too late for that. My brother's missing."

Wonderful. Missing kitty cases are never fun. You could work your tail off trying to find somebody and be outdone by a stupid "Have you seen this Cat?" sign on a lamp post.

5

"OK, why don't we back up? What's your name?"

"Oh, I'm sorry. My name is Molasses. I live over there in that house, and – what are you laughing at?"

Her name was Molasses and she was wondering what I was laughing at. Humans shouldn't be allowed to name their pets. I made out ok, but there were way too many animals out there with ridiculous names. When they needed a name for the kitty, did they go look in their pantry and pick the first thing that they saw? "Nothing. I wasn't laughing. What's your brother's name and what does he look like?"

"His name is Butterscotch." She paused for a second to see if I was going to start giggling. I held it together and she continued, "He's an American shorthair. He's about 10 pounds with short hair. He has a perfect thirty point face and he's mostly white with thick grey stripes in a Mackerel Tabby pattern."

"Is anybody else looking for him?"

She thought about that for a second. "Well our owners

are really going crazy looking for him and I told those dogs that patrol the neighborhood, but nobody seems to be getting anywhere."

"When was the last time you saw him?"

"Last week. It was the day before the weekend. We're not supposed to go out, but he knew how to leave the house when he wanted to. He'd go out at least once a week"

"And where was he going?"

"I don't know. We were close, but he would have to have his alone time. Only this time he didn't come back."

"Could he be going to see a girlfriend?"

"No, that I would know about. He was probably just going to gamble at that awful alley – Did you hear that?"

I had heard a dog bark that I didn't recognize. A minute or so before, I'd gotten a whiff of some strange dogs but there was no threat in sight.

"We're okay. Do you have any reason to think that

7

somebody took him?"

"No. There was no trouble at home between our people. We had no – Who are they?"

There were three dogs crossing the street coming towards us. Mean looking pit bulls, if that doesn't go without saying. They were going for rough, tough and menacing and I have to give them credit, they were getting the job done. I couldn't take one of them down, let alone all three.

I gave Molasses more credit. She didn't scream or bolt. She just stood her ground and glanced from me to them.

"Hey, pretty kitty" The lead dog said. "We came to ugly you up. You and your little boyfriend there." His buddies just growled. I could think of at least five good comebacks to that but as Yoshi has often told me, I need to select the proper time and place for smartaleck remarks. With three murderous killing machines a couple of yards away from us, I was going to need to use my head to do more than come up with witticisms.

CHAPTER 2

The three Pit Bulls were all growling and there was no doubt that if they got us, we'd be ripped to shreds. I whispered to Molasses, "Head up the tree! Now!"

There was a huge, towering evergreen tree fifteen feet behind us. Molasses instantly spun around and headed for it. The dogs bolted towards us. I let my instincts take over. My back went up, my tail went straight up and fluffed up and I let go with a hiss louder than I thought I was capable of. The dogs stopped dead in their tracks, long enough for Molasses to make it to the tree. Yoshi had told me that the meaner a bully, the more easily frightened they were. I spun around and headed after Molasses. They were right on top of me, but I had enough of a head start that I could leap for the tree before they could catch me. I did feel the snip of a dog's teeth just barely touching my tail. Then I was heading up the tree with the three dogs barking and jumping up the trunk, unable to climb after me. Molasses was waiting for me on a high limb. I joined her and we both ran across a branch and then jumped down to the roof of the house.

I heard the front door of the house open and a man's voice yelled, "Hey you dogs, get on out of here!" There was another barrage of angry barks and the door slammed.

At this point we were safely on the roof. She looked at me "Well, I guess you proved me wrong for laughing when you said you could be a bodyguard. I can't believe the way you held off those three killers by yourself!"

"Yeah, my girlish screams held them off long enough for us to escape."

"Whatever! That had to be the bravest thing I've ever seen in my life!" She seemed genuinely impressed. "Let me know what you find out!" She got a running start and then jumped over to roof of the next house. After doing the same for a couple of other houses, she was gone.

It then occurred to me that when she said that was the bravest thing she'd ever seen, I should've replied "You ain't seen nothing yet, baby" or something cool like that. Oh well, I wouldn't want to thrill her too much on our first meeting. Always leave them wanting more.

The next morning was a Monday. The people that I lived with had been home for two days straight and spent the morning dazed and frantic, trying to get out of the house for work and school. This was a hilarious sight that I usually looked forward to but I was a little short on sleep so I napped through it all. They were usually gone by 8:00. A few minutes after 9:00, I was going over the previous nights events with Yoshi. We were in the master bedroom where Yoshi liked to take his morning nap. He had his sixteen pound body perched on the woman's pillow as if it were his own. I was sitting on the floor next to the bed

11

looking up at him. Yoshi was completely black from head to tail, except for a few white hairs on his chest and his bright yellow eyes. His eyes were almond shaped and had been so prominent when he was a kitten that they made him look like a Siamese cat which is why our owners had given him an Asian name. As he grew, the resemblance to a Siamese cat went away but he kept the name. I never knew why they had named me "Gatsby", although I know that there's a famous book titled, "The Great Gatsby". I've always assumed that everybody just understood how great I am and they gave me a name to match. Yoshi's always saying that if they had given me a better name that I might have a humbler attitude.

I'd told Yoshi everything that happened last night from Percy's request to our beautiful client's missing brother to being chased by the gang of pit bulls. Although he looked sleepy, I knew he was paying attention to every detail. He always waited until I was finished to ask his questions. "What on earth does that dog want from me?" he asked.

"I don't know. Knowing him, it's probably some kind of criminal activity. We should just blow him off and concentrate on Mo's case."

"Mo?" His left eyebrow whiskers rose.

"I mean Molasses. Miss Molasses. Our new client, who I am treating with the utmost respect and professionalism." I smiled my cutest cat smile.

He sighed. "You're not getting overly familiar with a client again, are you? Has your collar even dried yet from all the tears you cried when that Siamese dumped you last week? And it was just last month that you were acting heartbroken when that Gwendolyn moved away."

"Look, I'm a professional. I'm not going to ask her to marry me until I've found her brother. Now, are you going to lay up there and comment on my love life all morning or do you have instructions?"

"Of course. First, you can stress to Percy that I'm not visiting him so any communication will need to go through you. I would've thought that everyone in the

13

neighborhood would know that by now, but apparently not. On the Butterscotch matter, you'll need to make the usual inquiries. Also, talk to Duke and see if he knows anything about those thugs that attacked you last night. They give an interesting twist to what should be a routine missing pet case."

"Twist? What twist? They were a bunch of thugs that thought they'd bully a couple of innocent cats."

He glanced at the alarm clock on the end table next to the bed. It was 9:52. Eight minutes until the mid-morning nap. Yoshi's mid-morning nap was not to be interrupted, postponed or cancelled for any reason short of the end of the world and even then under protest. I had to hurry him up. "Do you have any instructions that might actually help find this missing cat?"

"Do I really need to instruct you on that? It's going to be a pain, although Molasses did say something that might make things go easier although I need to think about that for a little while. In the meantime, you're going to have to canvas the area for a couple miles, asking every animal you encounter if they've seen him. Get help from your rat friend if you must and –"

He was interrupted by a flurry of barking coming from the side of the house. We both ran from the bedroom and went downstairs to the kitchen. Actually I ran. Yoshi walked after me. The kitchen window was half open and I could jump up on the windowsill to see what was going on. The window looked out on the house next door and the grass in-between. Sitting on the grass and barking at us was Duke, a 75 pound German Shepherd.

I greeted him. "Hey Duke."

"Hiya, kid." He had a gruff personality but was usually friendly to me. "I need you to-"

The words were hardly out of his mouth before Yoshi had jumped on the windowsill next to me and interrupted. "We don't work for you! Shouldn't you be out harassing the mailman?"

"Its ten o'clock. Shouldn't you be unconscious?"

Yoshi's schedule was well known. "I didn't come to see you; I need to talk with Gatsby." Duke said in a deep growl. His gruff personality usually got a lot gruffer when Yoshi was around.

Yoshi didn't care for Duke either and from the look on his face, he was about to tell Duke exactly what he thought of him. Then he yawned. It was ten o'clock. He jumped down off the windowsill, told me to "Handle it." and trotted back to the bedroom.

I looked back at Duke. "So, what can I do for you?"

"I need to show you something. Can you take a walk with me?"

"Sure, but I'm not bringing my pooper scooper."

"Come on. Let's go!" This time the deep growl was for me. Duke was not noted for his appreciation of dog humor. I went outside to join him.

Duke had been in the police K-9 corps for five years and after being injured in the line of duty had been forced to retire to the suburbs. He set himself and three other dogs up as the cops of the neighborhood. They patrolled and performed duties like harassing suspicious strangers, keeping feral animals away and stopping pets from pooping on the sidewalks. Yoshi and I were both super secret special honorary members of Duke's police force. Duke wanted us to become full members but we had declined. We were a little too independent minded to be expected to follow orders.

"Where are we going?" I said when I caught up to him.

"Not far." Was all the answer I got. He trotted off over the lawn and up the sidewalk with me right on his heels. It was a very nice day for mid-October with a warm temperature and a sunny sky. Some of the houses had Jack O'Lanterns on their porches and Halloween decorations in their windows. Yoshi always found the black cat decorations to be horribly offensive. At this time of the day most people were at work so that the streets were clear and everything was quiet. After we'd gone a couple of blocks in silence, Duke looked back at me and said, "So kid, I heard you had a little dust-up last night."

"How did you hear about that?"

"The night has a thousand eyes, kid. A little bird told me about three tough pit bulls being backed off by a little orange cat. I only know of one orange cat around here with that much nerve."

"OK, I'll admit to that. They came from out of nowhere. I had never seen those dogs before. Do you know anything about them?"

"No. But I have heard a rumor about dogfighting in the area."

That took me by surprise. "Dogfighting? Get out! Not in this neighborhood!"

"Crime has no area code, kid."

Yes, he actually talked like that. I didn't know exactly what the injury was that made him retire, but when he said things like that I suspected that had something to do with his head.

"OK", I said. "Where do I go to find this dogfighting?"

"If I knew that, I'd have shut them down by now!" He growled.

"Of course. Well, if I run into them again, I'll follow them to wherever they came from and let you know."

His head snapped around. "If you see them again, you run and get me quick!" He paused and looked up. "Here we are. Follow me."

We had stopped outside a two-story grey house.

The second-in-command of the Dog Patrol was Preston, another big bodied German Shepherd who was a little bigger than Duke but he was less muscular and more fat. He was sitting next to a smoke-grey cat who had obviously just been through a rough time. The cat was bruised, battered and beaten. His left eye was swollen shut, his right ear was cut and there were claw marks on his back and his chest. Other than that he looked good. Despite his injuries, he stood up straight and tall and had a regal attitude, like he owned the place.

As we approached I gave Preston a nod. He nodded back. I looked at the grey cat. "What happened, man? You look like I feel."

He responded "Well, if you're Gatsby you're the one who should look like this."

"Excuse me?"

Preston spoke up "Why don't we back up and make introductions? Then we can talk about why he looks like this." Preston was usually a voice of reason. "Gatsby, this little guy's name is Smokey. Smokey, you were right, this is Gatsby. Now why don't you tell Gatsby what you told me and the chief?"

"Fine I'll talk to the fleabag."

I spoke "That's nice, but how about you do it without the name-calling?"

Smokey was still scowling at me. "I was minding my own business last night and these three dogs jumped on me. I couldn't get away, they had me surrounded. After they beat me down, they asked me if I knew a cat named Gatsby. I said no and they told me to find him and tell him to back off."

I knew the answer to my next question but I asked it anyway. "Back off of what?"

"I don't know. I don't know who you are or who those dogs are or why they almost beat me to death or why I have to be your messenger boy."

"Can you describe these dogs?"

He did and there was no doubt about it, they were the same dogs that harassed me earlier last night. They must have come across this poor sucker after I got away from them. Looking at his bruises I felt kind of bad. Duke and Preston were both staring at me.

Duke spoke. "Well, kid? We're dealing with an assault here and I can't believe that it had anything to do with a missing kitty. I'm going to need you to tell me all about any other cases you're working on."

This put me in a weird spot. We really didn't have any other cases and I could just tell him that but the state of

21

our business affairs was none of Duke's business. On the

other hand, Duke was one of the only creatures in the

world that I didn't like to annoy for absolutely no reason. I

thought for a couple of seconds and decided if I told him

that I wasn't working on anything else he wouldn't believe

me anyway so why bother?

"Sorry, Duke" I said, "I got nothing for you."

"C'mon, kid". His tone had somehow slipped from

gruff but friendly to just plain gruff. I knew that it was

nothing personal but he thought that there was a

possibility that I knew something that he didn't and that

went against his natural order of things.

"Look, you know me well enough to know that I'm not

going to want to answer your question, right?"

Duke stayed silent. He wasn't going to play my game.

Preston was more accommodating and answered my

question.

"Right."

"Thanks." I continued. "Now knowing that, what

would I say if I had another case that would explain the beating that was inflicted on this poor soul?"

"You'd say that you didn't ." said Preston in a matter-of-fact tone of voice.

"Correct! Outright denial. Now, what would I say if I actually had no other cases?"

"You'd also deny it." Preston replied. "Especially if you were a smartaleck little jerk."

"Yeah, especially if I was a – Hey!" Despite Preston's insult, I continued. "Now, I really don't see how you guys expect me to-"

I stopped in mid-sentence. A little Scottie dog was approaching. His name was Rowdy and he was another one of Duke's officers. The snotty one. It was my theory that he was constantly acting like a tough guy to make up for his small stature. He didn't like me because of a move I'd made back when we were all searching for a missing garden gnome and he was the type that held a grudge.

"Hey, boss!" he yelled as he ran up to us. "You gotta

come with me! I found –" He stopped abruptly when he saw me.

"What? What is it?" Duke said. He usually wasn't that short with his guys, but he was still annoyed with me.

"Can we talk in private?" Rowdy spoke without taking his eyes off of me. "Let's go over there."

Duke rolled his eyes but agreed. He looked at me and Smoky. "You two stay right here." He Preston and Rowdy went over to the other side of the patio and had a conference in low tones.

Smokey and I stayed in place and tried to listen to what the dogs were discussing. No luck. So I turned to Smokey and said, "I need to talk to you. Where can I find you later?"

He was still hostile. "Look punk, if I felt better I'd love to meet you alone and pay you back for these bruises."

I tried to charm him. "C'mon my friend. I didn't put those bruises on you and I'm sorry you got caught up in whatever is going on. Can't we just have a nice conversation and maybe I can help get the guys that did this to you?"

"Whatever. Why can't we just wait until the dogs leave. They look like they're about to take off."

"Yeah and I'm going to have to follow them. Wherever they're going has something to do with me."

"How do you know that?"

"Well, the little dog isn't that smart." I explained, "You saw how he shut up as soon as he saw me."

"So," Smokey replied, "Maybe its super secret doggie patrol stuff."

"Nah. He saw you and he kept talking. He saw me and he clammed up. They're definitely talking about me."

Smokey didn't say anything so I continued. "If it had been Preston, he wouldn't have stopped talking when he saw me, he would've lied about what he wanted Duke for and told him later when I wasn't around."

"I guess you don't like that little dog."

"You guess right"

"And I guess you like yourself a whole lot."

"I can't help it. I'm a likable kind of cat. It might be contagious. I notice that you've spoken to me twice now without calling me a name. Be that as it may, you and I need to chat."

He rolled his eyes. "I'll be at the tree stump tonight. We can talk there. It looks like the convention is breaking up."

Duke, Preston and Rowdy had stopped talking and were staring at me. "Hey kid." Duke said, "We gotta go. You and me are going to talk later."

"Where are you going?" I asked.

"Dog Patrol business." He answered. "Don't worry about it."

"Can I tag along?" I asked casually. I knew what the likely answer to that was, but they would expect me to ask.

"No need," Duke said. "It's got nothing to do with you."

"Fine. Go ahead, I'll just stay here and have a talk with Smokey." I said in a tone that implied that that was exactly

what I wanted to do anyway and that I had somehow
tricked them into leaving me alone with Smokey.

"Good." Duke said. "I'll come see you and Yoshi later."
He and the other dogs trotted to the driveway on their way
to the front of the house.

I counted to ten, gave Smokey a wink and then took off
after the dogs.

CHAPTER 3

I followed the dogs for five blocks. They took the sidewalks for the first two blocks until they saw an old man mowing his lawn. If he got a look at three unaccompanied dogs strolling down the sidewalk, he'd probably decide that a call to Animal Control was in order. The only animal control Duke and his boys believed in was the kind that they provided. So they took to travelling through backyards, hopping over and going under fences when necessary. This was ideal for me since there were lots of trees, shrubs and playground equipment for me to duck behind as I trailed the dogs. Duke would occasionally turn and look back to see if anybody was following but he didn't spot me. It was his highly trained police dog eyes against my natural feline stealth. I scored a point for feline stealth as we approached what I assumed was our destination. The last backyard fence that the dogs jumped led to a lot behind an abandoned gas station.

The subdivision that we all lived in was bordered on the east by a major six lane street that was packed with supermarkets, fast food restaurants and gas stations. The street functioned as a sort of a barrier for the neighborhood animals as very few of us were insane enough to try crossing a busy six lane highway. This particular gas station had been closed for awhile. They had opened up a newer sleeker quickie mart across the street and I guess that this spot was going to be abandoned until the humans decided what kind of greasy fast food they wanted to sell from this location. In the meantime there was an empty medium sized building with a garage bay and a couple of raised platforms in front where the gas pumps once stood. The whole lot was paved but there were some weeds popping up through the cracks in the asphalt. While lots of cars were constantly passing by the front of the place, the back was pretty quiet. That was where Duke, Preston and Rowdy had stopped. I hadn't jumped over the last fence, so I was in a backyard looking for a good vantage point. There was a nice big oak tree close to the fence that I could sit behind, hear everything and stick my head out every now again to see what was happening with little chance of the dogs seeing me.

Duke and his boys were about forty feet away from me. I was sure that they wouldn't be able to see me and since the wind was blowing towards me, I was pretty sure that they wouldn't be able to smell me either.

The dogs were just sitting in the middle of the lot waiting for something. They all looked tense. Which I suppose made me tense. Which is probably why I just about jumped out of my skin when a voice from behind me whispered, "Hello".

A lesser cat would've screeched and jumped fifteen feet in the air. Not me. My tail merely puffed up to five or six times its normal size. The voice belonged to Molasses. Of course.

"Did I scare you?" she whispered, seeing the inflated state of my tail.

"Nah, It's a new style. I used the blow dryer on my tail all morning. It's what all the cool kittens are doing." I thought that it would be a good time to change the subject. "What are you doing here?"

"I live around here. I was sitting in the back window and I saw those dogs go through my backyard and then you went by. I thought that you might be working on my problem."

"No, not right now-" I broke off what I was about to say because I saw her eye widen as she saw something going on behind me.

I turned around to see that Duke and company had been joined by three other dogs. It was the pit bulls that Mo and I had encountered last night. I was immediately annoyed with myself for being distracted and not seeing where they had come from. Yoshi was never going to let me hear the end of this.

Things were starting to happen with the dogs. "My name is Duke." Duke announced. "This neighborhood is my jurisdiction. Who are you?"

The leader of the pit bulls smiled. She was in a much better mood than last night. "I don't have time for introductions. Your little punk dog said that you wanted to talk to me. What do you want?"

Molasses whispered to me, "Wow. Aren't they even going to sniff each other?"

"No, they skipped the traditional butt-sniffing greeting. This is as serious as heartworm."

Duke continued, "OK, if that's how you want it. Here's the deal – my guys and I enforce the law around here. My name's Duke. This is Preston and this is Rowdy. Now, if you-"

He was cut off by the obnoxious snickering coming from the pit bulls. Like a good soldier Duke carried on. "We keep this neighborhood nice for the people and animals that live here. So when I hear rumors about dog fighting in a nice place like this, I get interested. You guys know anything about that?"

"Oh, I get it," The leader of the pit bulls said, "You see a bunch of pit bulls and all of sudden, you start asking us about dog fighting. That's discrimination!" Her two friends stood behind her and snickered menacingly.

"What's your name, lady?" Duke growled.

"I'm Nails." She nodded her head towards her two friends. "This is Seven and his name's Nine. And yeah, that's their names not their ages."

Those names started Molasses giggling. I shushed her. She was beautiful but she didn't seem to have a lot of self-control.

"Anything else?" Nails asked Duke.

"Oh, just a few questions. Where do you live? Where do you come from? What's your owner's name? Are you in the neighborhood for a visit or do you think that you're going to be here permanent? What do you know about

33

dogfights? You answer those in order you'd like."

A mean smile was on her scarred lips. "I don't like answering in any order. I don't care about you and your silly doggie scout patrol. I'm not answering anything!"

Nobody said anything for a few seconds. Then Duke spoke. "OK, if that's how you want it. This get together was your idea. Why don't you tell me what it is you want to say?"

"Nothing" She replied. "We heard you were looking for us and I wanted to meet you and get it out of the way. I got nothing to say to you and as far as I'm concerned, you punks have no authority over me and my crew!"

"Listen to me," Duke said, "I'm not impressed by your attitude. If you or anybody with you is doing anything illegal, my boys and I will shut it down. Believe it!"

"Oh please, you and your boys can't even secure a secret meeting. Who's that behind that tree?"

I looked at Molasses. "She's talking about us." I whispered, "Your giggling gave us away."

"It did not!" she said, "It was your shushing. You shush too loud, you giggle shusher!"

"Giggle-shusher! That's the worst kind of shusher! How dare you call me a –"

"Excuse me." Duke's angry voice rang out. "Come out from behind that tree!"

Mo and I stepped out from the tree. All six dogs on the other side of the chain link fence were staring at us. Duke and Rowdy were enraged, Preston rolled his eyes and the pit bulls looked like they wanted to eat us.

"It's those stupid cats from last night!" said Nails. Then she said a word I'd rather not repeat.

"Hey, watch your mouth," I said. "There's a lady present and I ain't talking about you!"

To look at her, you wouldn't think that that was the meanest thing anybody had ever said to her, but she acted like it was. Her scarred face actually looked like her feelings had been hurt for half of a second and then it turned mean again as she turned to the dog called Nine

35

and barked, "Get them!"

Fast as lightning he bolted a couple of steps and then jumped over the fence that separated us from the dogs. Duke and his dogs started to follow him but Nails and Seven jumped in front of them, barking and snapping. That was all I saw of them before my common sense forced me to turn and run. Molasses was a few steps ahead of me and since she knew this area better than I did, I just followed her.

She ran back to the front of the house that we had been behind and made a beeline up the street. She seemed to know where she was going so I decided to trust her and just follow her lead. I just hoped that she wouldn't climb a tree. Nothing is more embarrassing than being chased up a tree. Especially when the Fire Department has to be called to get you down. My heart sank when I saw that she was headed straight for a Douglas Fir. It was very young tree in the middle of a very well maintained front yard. It couldn't have been any taller than five feet and if we climbed it all

Nine would have to do is jump moderately high to sink his

teeth into us. Following Molasses was starting to seem like

a bad idea but at that point, we were all running at full

speed and there weren't a lot of other options. Molasses

leapt up to the top of the tree. As she was in the air, I

finally realized what she was doing. She was brilliant! As

she landed on the top, the whole tree bent forward under

her weight until she and the treetop were on the ground.

The tree strained to get itself upright but Molasses weighed

a little too much for it. I had only been a couple steps

behind her so I jumped forward, leaping over both

Molasses and the bent tree. Nine had been a couple steps

behind me and thankfully had only been paying attention

to my behind. Seeing me jump, he also jumped forward.

With expert timing, Molasses stepped off of the treetop as

soon as I had passed over her. It sprang back to its vertical

position with enough force and power that it hit Nine right

in his face and chest and knocked him into the air. He

flipped three times and landed twenty feet away into the

hedges of the house next door. Molasses and I kept running and there was no way the he was going to be able to catch up. As we ran we could hear the gradually fading sounds of Nine cussing, yelling and vowing that he was going to get us. We had gone about three blocks before we couldn't hear him anymore. We sat on the sidewalk and panted for a bit, then I looked over at Molasses and said, "I think I'm in love. Every time I see you, my heart beats faster, I get an adrenaline rush and I pant like crazy."

"That's nice," She replied, "But I think I just met a dog that's head over heels in love with me."

As I laughed, she winked at me and trotted home.

CHAPTER 4

I got home at about 1:00. I had checked in with my bird
contacts and asked them to keep an eye out for
Butterscotch. I desperately needed a nap but I was going
to have to report to Yoshi before I could get any sleep.
Our humans wouldn't be home until at least 5:30 or maybe
6:00 if I was lucky. Three or four hours of sleep would
have to do.

When I walked into the house, I saw Maury the mouse
coming through the living room. Maury was an operative
that we used when the workload required more than just
me. Yoshi must have called him in.

"Hey Maury," I said as I repressed a desire to attack and
eat him.

"G-Gatsby! How are you?" He squeaked nervously. I

assumed that the nervousness had to do with the fact that he knew that I was suppressing a desire to attack and eat him. I get that a lot from mice and birds.

"So what's going on? You get a job from Yoshi?"

"Yep." He said, "I'm just coming from meeting with him."

"What's he got you doing?"

I knew what he was going to say before he did. If Yoshi had called him in without telling me, it was for something that I wasn't supposed to know about.

"Uh, I'm really sorry but he gave me strict instructions not to tell anybody anything. Sorry." It looked like he was genuinely pained to tell me this.

"I don't think that would include me, his partner."

Maury gulped. "Um. Especially you. I'm sorry."

Maury was afraid of me but he still wasn't going to tell me what was going on. Continuing the conversation was pointless.

"Whatever." I dismissed him and trotted off towards

the stairs. He sighed and then went off on his top-secret mission.

I found Yoshi in the home office. He was reading. Our man had a variety of different kinds of books on a couple of seven foot tall bookshelves and Yoshi would help himself. He knew how to read and would knock books off of the bookshelf during the afternoon. The people assumed that the books fell off when we were climbing up the shelves. Today Yoshi was reading something about the Civil War. Fascinating.

"I'm back." I announced.

He lifted the whiskers over his left eye. "You've been gone for three hours. That must have been some conversation."

"It was more than conversation; I've had a very eventful morning." I said. "Do I report now or can I get some sleep?"

Yoshi considered this. He had his faults but he genuinely hated to keep any cat from sleep. Although he didn't hate it that much because his next words were: "I think it would be better if you reported now. You'll have time for a nap."

So I told Yoshi everything that had happened since I'd left that morning. He sat on his haunches and listened without interrupting. When I had finished I let loose with a huge yawn, just to emphasize the point that some cats hadn't been in bed all morning.

It didn't matter. He had comments and questions. His first question was one that I had been hoping that he would skip.

"Which direction did the pit bulls come from?"

I cleared my throat then answered, "I believe that I mentioned that I didn't see where they came from. I was speaking with our client."

He rolled his eyes, which is a good trick for a cat. If you don't believe me ask your cat. Just asking that question will probably make him try but odds are that he won't be able to do it.

"So you were too preoccupied by this girl to observe vital information?"

"Oh, come on!" I protested. "I knew that you wouldn't be happy but aren't you overdoing it? How is that vital information?"

He looked at me like someone who is being very patient with a very slow child. "Duke suspects that these dogs are involved with dog fighting, doesn't he?"

"Yeah, from the way they look you don't have to be Sherlock Holmes to make that deduction. What does that have to do with a missing cat?" As those words were coming out of my mouth, I suddenly realized what he was getting at. "Oh!"

A couple of months ago Yoshi had told me stories about dogfighting and how it was controlled by vicious, nasty people who had no regard for animal life. There were stories about housepets being kidnapped and forced to fight dogs either as a training method for the pit bulls or to make the dogs more bloodthirsty. Yoshi had told me about this in an effort to get me to be more careful when I went outside the house.

I usually ignore stories like this because Yoshi was full of horrible stories of the bad things that humans do to animals. Usually at this time of the year, he would go on and on about his belief that every Halloween, devil worshipping teenagers would abduct black cats and hurt them while trying to practice witchcraft. I get around a lot and I read the newspaper but I've never actually heard of anything like this happening. When I try to tell that to Yoshi, he just sniffs and talks about how everybody hates black cats and cover-up the crimes committed against them. For most of October not only will he not go outside but he'll stay away from windows at nights and weekends for fear that some crazed teenager will see him and abduct him to use in some weird ritual.

So I'd never known how seriously to take his "pets being kidnapped to be sparring partners for pit bulls" story. Maybe as serious as a case of heartworm.

"So you think that he got kidnapped and is being used to train dogfighters?" I asked.

"I don't know. But if we can find out where these dogs are living, we can determine whether or not Butterscotch is there. At the least, we can have Duke shut them down. The thought that there might be dogfights going on in this neighborhood sickens me."

I considered that for a minute. "So is that what I'm supposed to do tonight? Track those dogs down?"

"Yes, talk with the cats that live in the area around that gas station."

"Got it. Anything else?" There was always something else.

"Yes. Have Molasses here at 11:30 tomorrow morning. Assuming she can tell time."

"Really?"

"Yes, I have a few questions that I'd like to ask her myself. I also want to meet the woman who has you in such a state that you can't even tell me a simple thing like

45

from which direction a pack of vicious dogs came from."

This would have been an ideal time to roll my eyes if I could. I couldn't so I just asked if there was anything else.

"I also would like to talk to that other cat, Smoky. Please arrange for him to come here tomorrow at about noon. That's all. Go get some sleep."

"On my way," I said, "But I have one question for you. I saw Maury leaving. Is he doing anything that I need to know about?"

"No." That was all he said. He had gone back to his book.

"Well if that's how it's going to be, fine. I'm going to sleep." I turned around and trotted to the sweet bliss of the living room couch.

"One more thing." He stopped me in my tracks just as I'd reached the doorway.

"What?" I said.

"Did you find out what Percy wanted?"

"Nope. He was locked in his house when I went by this

morning. Maybe I'll see him tonight."

Yoshi shook his head. "Your priority tonight is finding out where those dogs live. Percy will wait."

"You got it." I said. Then I yawned and headed off to dreamland.

CHAPTER 5

I'm going to skip ahead to the next day. The previous night I had arranged with Molasses to be at our house at 11:30. Then I had seen Smoky and he'd promised to show up at noon, although he still had a very nasty attitude. I had gotten nowhere asking the neighborhood cats if they knew anything about the pit bulls or dogfights. Cats are usually keen observers of everything, especially things involving dogs but in this case no cat seemed to know anything.

So it was 11:30 on Halloween morning and Yoshi was perched on the kitchen windowsill waiting for our appointment with Molasses. I was outside, sitting in the grass about six feet away from the window. The weather was ok for late October, with grey skies and only a slight chill in the air. The human children should be able to trick or treat tonight without having to wear coats over their costumes.

At 11:35 Molasses appeared. She walked up and sat down beside me. Yoshi looked down on us from the bay window.

I did the introductions. "Molasses, this is Yoshi. Yoshi, Molasses."

"Hi." She said.

"Hello." He replied. "Unfortunately I don't have any news of your brother. I had a couple of questions that I wanted to ask you directly."

She smiled. "Shoot."

Yoshi started with standard questions that went over stuff that I had already covered with her. Did Butterscotch have any enemies? Was he likely to run away? He asked a bunch of other questions that made me think that this was a waste of time. Then he asked something that I thought was completely from out of left field: "Is your brother a participant in cat shows?"

I thought that he'd run out of questions and was just fishing around but she answered in the affirmative. "Yes," she said "He's a show cat. He's great too. He's taken first place in his breed at the last three shows he's competed in."

Yoshi stopped to consider this information. I jumped in with my own question. "Are there any shows coming up?"

"Sure, there's one next week at the convention center."

I followed up. "Do you think that his disappearance might have anything to do with the cat show?"

She laughed. "Do you mean that he got stage fright and ran away? No, he's a very confident cat. He always assumes that he's going to win. He wouldn't run off because of that."

Yoshi spoke up. "I don't think that's what Gatsby had in mind. He was probably thinking of something more sinister. Does Butterscotch have any rivals at the cat shows?"

"Rivals, you mean like enemies?" She said as if she were shocked by the question. "I think that you guys have the wrong impression of cat shows. It's a great atmosphere. We're all friends."

I could tell by the look on his face that Yoshi wasn't buying that. "I'm sorry. I admit that I don't know a lot about cat shows but my knowledge of feline nature makes me believe that a cat show would be a hotbed of treachery and backstabbing."

Molasses smiled at him. "I like the way you talk." she said, "I'm not sure that you're saying much but it sounds good. What do you mean by feline nature?"

"We cats are part of a species that include the animal kingdom's most perfect hunters, the world's most brutally efficient fighters and most of us are shrewd, resourceful and sharp-witted. With all of these gifts it's not surprising that we can also be a little arrogant, self-righteous and stubborn. Especially towards each other. I find it unbelievable that these strong inborn characteristics don't emerge during a competition."

She thought about that for a moment and then said, "Is that what you guys tell yourselves to get through the day? That you're really panthers and lions? You may not have heard, but housecats have been domesticated for thousands of years. As far as I'm concerned we are warm, friendly and completely loveable. "

Apparently Yoshi didn't feel like arguing. "Whatever. Can you tell Gatsby the names and homes of Butterscotch's rivals at the cat show?"

The smile came back to her face. "Sure, but we'd have to start with me."

"Is that so?"

"Yes, I've come in second to him in the last four shows we've been in."

"How did you feel about that?" Yoshi asked.

"I wasn't happy about it. But I haven't done away with him or anything"

"Did your owners treat you any differently since he was

always the winner?"

She snorted. "No, if anything they spent more time with me, trying to get me over the hump."

"Could he have run away, thinking that you were going to beat him?"

"No. Absolutely not. He goes into these shows believing without a doubt that he's the best cat. He's not the type that feels threatened."

"Is there anyone else that he might consider a threat?" Yoshi asked.

"No. There are other cats that compete with us, but he wouldn't consider them threats. He thinks very highly of himself."

"I suppose so. I'd still like you to tell Gatsby about any other rival cats in these shows. Now, I have an appointment in a few minutes. Do you have any questions for me?"

"Actually I do. I have a question for you and your uncharacteristically quiet friend here." She nodded in my direction. I returned the nod and she continued. "Gatsby hasn't mentioned anything about payment. And the other pets that I talked to about you guys said that you didn't charge for your services. Is that right?"

"Mostly." Yoshi said. "Although we've been known to keep a portion if we recover something delicious. We mostly work *pro bono*"

She looked puzzled. "For bones? That sounds more like what a dog would charge."

No. Pro Bono is a latin term. It means gratis-," he stopped himself and started over. "It means for free. We mostly work for free."

"Why? What's in it for you?"

I could tell from the look on Yoshi's face that, despite what he had just said about having an appointment in a few minutes, we were in for a speech.

"Well let's go back to what I said about feline nature. Gatsby and I are hunters by nature but the life of a housecat provides very little in the way of prey. Our needs for food and shelter are satisfied but at the expense of our instinctual need to hunt. This could result in boredom. So to fight our boredom, we try to solve problems for the pets in our neighborhood."

At that point I felt the need to speak up. "Of course one of us can only heed our hunting instincts when they're not during our regularly scheduled naptimes or mealtimes or if we're not reading or if we never have to leave the house or do anything that might make us uncomfortable -"

"That's enough." Yoshi hissed. "What happened to you being uncharacteristically quiet?"

I just grinned at him so he turned to Molasses and said, "Miss Molasses, I'm afraid that I have another meeting. If you don't mind, Gatsby will escort you to the front of the house and I'm sure you can find your way home from there."

"Can't he walk me home?"

I tried to look apologetic. "Sorry kid, I'm needed here." As we walked to the front of the house I was able to get a few names and addresses of Butterscotch's rivals at the cat shows. I told her that I would have loved to walk her home but duty called. I watched her walk away until she was a couple blocks away. Then I went back to Yoshi.

Smokey was already there, sitting in the spot that I had vacated. He didn't look much better than he had the last time I'd seen him and the grimace on his face indicated that his attitude wasn't any better either. He and Yoshi were already talking but something else grabbed my attention. I had glanced over my shoulder and noticed a tiny grey shape dart across our driveway and into the hedges. I was pretty sure that it Maury the mouse. The most likely reason that he would be out at this time of day is whatever secret mission he was doing for Yoshi. Was he following Molasses? Was he watching to see if someone else had been following Molasses? Was he looking out to warn us in case the pit bulls showed up? I didn't know the answers to any of those questions so I just sat down and told Smokey a lie.

"You're looking better.'" I said.

"Shut up!" He replied, friendly as ever.

Yoshi ignored Smokey's rudeness. "Smokey and I had just introduced ourselves. I was just telling him that he should really see a vet."

"Wow," I said, "You wouldn't tell your worst enemy to go to the vet."

Smokey growled, "The only way I'm going to a vet is if Animal Control snatches me. No thanks. I'll heal up fine eventually."

"Ah yes, the rigors of being a stray."

"How would a punk like you know, in your fancy house?"

Yoshi sighed. "I was on the streets for a few months in my youth. In some ways it was the best time of my life. If you envy my comfort, I envy your independence. Whatever!" He waved that topic away. "I called you here to ask you about the attack you suffered the other day. Can you tell me what happened?"

Smokey glared at me, apparently thinking that I hadn't told Yoshi what I had learned yesterday. Before I could open my mouth to defend myself, he spoke. "Well, I was over on Colston drive when those three pit bulls came at me."

"What was the nearest intersection?"

"What?"

"I'd like to know exactly where this took place."

"OK, it was two houses down from McKinley. Anyway, these dogs come from out of nowhere and had me surrounded!"

Yoshi looked impatient, "What do you mean 'from out of nowhere'? Which direction did they come from?"

"I don't know!" Smokey's usual enraged attitude had abated for a second and he seemed a little flustered. "It happened fast. I just looked up and they were all around me."

Yoshi didn't seem convinced of this. "You must be one incredibly self absorbed cat to not notice three pit bulls coming at you. Can you at least tell me if they all came from the same direction or from three different directions?"

"I don't know. What are you, an idiot? They were together; wouldn't they have all had to have come from the same direction?"

Yoshi sighed. "I suppose so. Then what happened?"

"The girl one told me to relax, that they weren't going to hurt me."

"Is that exactly what she said?"

"Yeah, but I didn't have my secretary there taking notes so who can be sure?"

Yoshi sighed again. "There's no need for sarcasm. I just want everything as factual as possible."

"Fine. That's what she said."

"What happened next?"

"Then she asked me if I knew a cat named Gatsby. I said no and she goes, 'Stop lying, all of you cats know each other. When you see Gatsby, tell him to mind his own business.' Then they gave me a beatdown." He looked at me. "So I figure I owe this jerk a beating."

I said, "You come look me up when your boo-boos are all better."

Yoshi spoke up. "I wouldn't recommend it. Gatsby may be smaller than you but he's quite a roughneck. Your issue seems to be more with these pit bulldogs than with him. Is there anything you can tell us that would help find them?"

"No. And I don't see what you could do about it anyway. You or that German Shepherd that thinks he's a cop."

"Maybe not. Let me ask you this: We have reason to believe that the dogs that attacked you are involved in dogfighting. Do you know anything about that?"

The question seemed to startle Smokey. He hesitated for a second, then answered. "What? They didn't say anything about dogfighting. I don't know anything about that."

DING! DING! DING! The lie detector in my head was going off. Yoshi's question had caught him off guard and his angry facade dropped for a minute. I didn't quite get how he could have had anything to do with a dogfighting ring but the way his attitude shifted from confusion to innocence to denial made me sure that he was lying.

If Yoshi agreed he wasn't showing it. "Fine. I believe I'm done. You don't have any questions, do you Gatsby?" His tone made it pretty clear that I'd better not. "Have a nice rest of your day."

Smokey looked up at Yoshi, then at me then back at Yoshi. He still seemed a little on edge from the dogfighting question but the anger was back. "Well that was a whole lot of nothing. Thanks for wasting my time!" With that Mr. Personality turned and trotted off towards the back of the house.

I must have been in a strange pose because Yoshi asked me. "What are you thinking of doing?"

I looked up at him. "I'm going to wait a couple of seconds and then follow him. Maybe we can salvage something out of dragging him here."

"No," Yoshi said, "That won't be necessary."

"What! How could it not be necessary? You know as well as I do that he was lying about not knowing anything about the dogfighting."

"Oh yes. But he knows you. If you try following him, he'll probably spot you."

I snorted. "Oh please. Nobody spots me."

"I'm well aware of your abilities, but why take chances? Why don't you go take a nap?"

"Look I'm a cat of action. Unlike you, I only need four or five naps a day."

"Ah, to be young and annoying." Yoshi answered, and then he let loose with a massive yawn. "You're four years old. When you're nine like me, you'll appreciate the importance of rest. Since you have so much energy, why don't you go see what Percy wants?"

"What?"

"Percy the bulldog? Remember him?"

"Yeah I remember him. I thought we were going to

blow him off."

"Apparently you need something to do while we're awaiting developments on our other cases."

I smirked. "Does 'awaiting developments' mean that you don't know what to do next?"

"No. It means go see Percy and leave me alone." He turned so he could jump down from the windowsill and presumably go off to another nap.

"Hold on!" I said, "I've got a question to further my education in whatever it is that we do."

Yoshi sighed at having to put off his rest for another thirty seconds. "What is it?"

"Why did you ask Molasses about cat shows? I mean, that came out of nowhere but it was dead-on."

Yoshi sighed again. "It wasn't from out of nowhere. You need to pay more attention. You told me that Molasses had described her brother as having a thirty point face, didn't you?"

"Yes."

"That's not generally a common way to describe a cat. That's cat show talk. I'll see you when I wake up." With that he turned around and jumped down. I could hear him go "thump" on the kitchen floor and trot off to bed. I starting walking towards Percy's house wondering how in the world I was supposed to know how people talked at cat shows.

CHAPTER 6

I didn't go straight to Percy's. It had occurred to me that a nap might not be such a bad idea, so it wasn't until late afternoon that I set off to Percy's house. I didn't sleep that well as I spent a lot of time wondering why Yoshi hadn't let me follow Smokey. He obviously knew something about the dogfighting. Even though our main objective was finding Butterscotch, if we could get information on the dog fighting and shut it down, why not? Something about Smokey had annoyed me from the first time I met him. He didn't seem like any stray cat I had ever met. His coarse language was okay but his haughty attitude just seemed wrong. He always acted like he was the most important cat in the room, which isn't something that you would expect from a stray. Then there was his attitude towards me. He really didn't seem to like me at all. There really had to be something seriously wrong with him.

The good thing about Percy is that at this time of day you always knew where to find him. Late afternoon would find him chained in the backyard. The other good thing about Percy is that he was usually chained. His bark may be worse than his bite but who needs to test that theory?

I found him in his backyard, furiously barking at a toad. The toad was just beyond the reach of Percy's chain and was just sitting in the grass, unimpressed by Percy's histrionics.

"Yo, Percival!" I called. "What's up? You busy keeping dangerous prowlers at bay?"

"Well it's about time." he responded. Then he looked around. "Where's your boss?"

"Yoshi has better things to do. I wish I did. What do you want?"

"Well it's too late now!"

"Too late for what?" I impulsively responded. I instantly regretted having said that. I could've just accepted that I was too late and turned around and left. Nope, I had to ask.

"Too late to get me trained for the dogfights!"

Never mind what I just said about regretting my question. "What are you talking about?"

"I heard that there was going to be dog fights going down in the neighborhood tonight and we all know that I'm top dog around here! I —"

I had to interrupt. He would go on like that forever. "OK, so what does this have to do with Yoshi and me?"

"I wanted Yoshi to train me and be my manager!"

I would've laughed my tail off if I wasn't so keyed up that Percy might have some info on the dog fighting ring. Ever since we had chased away a giant rat that had been bullying him, Percy had gotten the idea that there was nothing that Yoshi couldn't do. I decided to try some logic.

"Don't humans run this dogfighting thing?"

"Yeah!"

"Do you actually you think that your owner's going to take you and put you in a fight?"

"What?" He thought about this for a minute. "Naw, he's too lame. We'll have to go by ourselves."

"I don't pretend to know how this stuff works, but you really think that they'll let you fight without an owner?"

"Uh, I don't know. They'll see how awesome I am and they'll have to put me in!"

"Then what?" I asked.

"Then I'm going to beat down some fool and make some money!"

"Do you think that the humans running this are going to give a dog money?"

He knew that I was getting at something but he wasn't getting it. Then a light seemed to go on in his empty head. "Oh, I get it." He said. "If Yoshi's my manager, I guess they would pay him. Talent like me shouldn't be handling the money."

I took a deep breath and let out a long deep cat sigh.
"Look there's three things wrong with your plan. Number
one is that nobody knows where these dog fights are so we
wouldn't be able to –"

"I know where they are!" He said indignantly.

"What? How?"

"Same way I found out about them in the first place.
This ugly girl and her two buddies were cutting through
my yard the other night so I told them to get moving. You
know the routine. They laughed at me 'cause I was tied
down with this stupid chain." He grimaced. "They told me
if I was really tough that I'd be at the dog fights on
Halloween and settle with them then."

I was getting impatient. "OK, so where is it?"

"They're in that abandoned brick house off of Sunbury."
His eyes narrowed. "Now are you guys going to help me
or not?"

"No. For two reasons now. Reason number one is that

you would get torn to shreds. Not that that would be so horrible but I don't want to have anything to do with it. Reason number two is that the humans who run this sick stuff are not going to let a dog enter by himself and if you win they're certainly not going to give you any money! These people exploit animals for profit and the only thing they're giving dogs is pain and misery!"

He looked at me with hard eyes and growled, "You better watch your tone, cat. Don't talk to me like I'm stupid. One of these days I'm not going to be chained to this house."

Which was a good point, but I couldn't resist asking him a question: "And how in the world were you planning to spend money? Were you going to walk into a store with a wad of cash in your mouth, go to the meat counter and ask for prime rib?"

He just glared at me. I walked away wondering what exactly he thought he was going to do with money.

CHAPTER 7

I took off immediately in the direction of the brick house that Percy had mentioned. I knew exactly where it was and it would only take ten minutes to get there. As I walked I tried to figure out what I was going to do when I got there. I wanted to make sure that it was the place where the dogfights were being held and if so, I wanted to see if they had Butterscotch and if so, I wanted to rescue him and take him to Molasses. That was a whole lot of "if so's". Anyway if I could tell for sure that the dogfights were operating out of that house, I could tell Duke and he could get his owner and the human police to shut them down. If you're out there reading this and you think that I should've went straight to Duke first, you're probably correct but that's not the way I do things.

On the south end of our subdivision, the backyards extended into woods. On the other side of these woods was a hill and on top of the hill was an old two story brick house that was at least a hundred and fifty years old. The house hadn't been lived in for a long time and looked awful. The windows had all been broken by rowdy children and the white paint on the windowframes and pillars was flaking. In spite of all this, the house still gave off a homey vibe. I had made it through the woods and was sitting behind a tree looking up at the house. I thought that I could hear barking. I decided to stop and think. If anybody was in the house looking out of a window, they might see me coming. The smart thing to do would be to leave and come back after dark. That way I could let Yoshi know what I'd found out and see if he had any ideas. He really hadn't contributed much to this affair so far.

At this point I was used to Molasses sneaking up behind me so I didn't react at all when she walked up behind me. In fact before she could say anything, I said, "What's new, pussycat? What are you doing here?"

"You passed by my house and you were moving fast. I thought maybe you had a lead on my brother, so I followed you."

Great. To get from Percy's to the brick house, I did have to pass through Molasses' neighborhood and I was so preoccupied that she must have followed me through the woods without me noticing. If Yoshi ever found out, here's another thing that I'd never hear the end of.

"So is Butterscotch in there?" she asked.

"I sure hope not." I replied. "I think that that's where they're having dogfights."

She shuddered. "Ew! That's gross!" The she gave me doubtful look. "I haven't heard of any dogfights around here. Are you sure?"

"Well my source of information is unreliable to say the least." I admitted. "But I see two cars and a truck in the driveway of a house that has been abandoned for as long as I've lived here."

She looked at the cars and the pickup truck that I had indicated. "That's probably people renovating the house."

"Could be."

"Do you think that Butterscotch is in there?" She asked.

"Is he good at interior design?"

"No smart guy, I mean that if that is in fact a house where they have dogfights do you think that Butterscotch is in there?"

"I don't know." I admitted.

"So what are you going to do?"

"I'm going to watch the house until I know what's going on. We call that surveillance."

"Good plan," she said. Then she started walking up the hill. "I don't have enough patience for surveillance. I'm going to go look in the windows." She said over her shoulder.

I ran after her. "Wait up. That's what I was going to do anyway. I just thought that you might be impressed with me if I used a big word like 'surveillance'."

We went around the hill so that we could approach the house from the windowless eastern side. Hopefully no windows meant that no one would see us coming.

Despite the vehicles in the driveway, the house still seemed deserted. The most prominent sound that we could hear was the leaves rustling as they blew over the grass but I was sure that I could hear a lot of angry barking coming from inside the house.

We had just gotten right up against the house when Mo commented, "Wow. A spooky old house. All we need is a black cat to make Halloween complete. So where's your buddy?"

"Keep your voice down," I whispered. "Yoshi wouldn't be caught dead outside of the house on Halloween. Well any night really, but especially Halloween."

We sat looked, listened and smelled for a few minutes but we weren't gaining any new information. "Wait here," I said. "I'm going to check things out."

I wasn't gone long. I just went around the house,

searching for any clues as to what was going on inside.

"Well?" Mo asked when I got back.

"There are definitely dogs in there."

I could smell that from down the hill. Anything else?"

"There's a barrel in the back. It collects water from the busted gutter for some reason. It's pretty full from that storm a couple of nights ago" I said.

She gave me a look.

"Nothing else." I admitted.

"Let's go in!" she said. She really was impatient. She walked over towards the front of the house and I followed.

"What? Do you want to get torn to shreds?"

"I want to find Butterscotch. How else are we going to know if he's in there?"

I tried to be a voice of reason. "We can stop and think of a way that doesn't involve certain death."

She stopped and looked up at a busted first floor window. "I'm going in that window. I know you're not a coward so let's go!"

I wasn't so sure of that but I wasn't going to let her know so we were going inside. I figured that our chances of getting back out were low but I wasn't going to have her think that I was a coward.

"OK then." I said. Oh boy.

The window that she's been talking about had a huge hole in the glass, probably made by some rock throwing boy. It was an easy way for us to gain entry to the house. As she crouched down to jump up to the windowsill, I tried one last attempt to be logical. "This is incredibly dangerous. I know that you're worried about your brother and that blood's thicker than water but –"

She stopped and looked at me. "Butterscotch and I aren't blood relatives. We've just lived together since we were kittens."

"You're roommates?"

"Well, we're good friends."

I didn't like the sound of that. I admit that I may have been feeling a little jealous. "How good?" I asked.

"Not as good as he wanted." She said as she got ready to jump.

"What does that mean?"

She sighed. "He's wanted to get romantic for years but I just think of him as my brother. Is now really a good time for this discussion? I'm going in!" With that she jumped up to the windowsill.

That had gone about as well as any other time that I had tried to be the voice of reason. I jumped up beside her and then we went through the broken window into the dark old house.

We seemed to be in the living room. Although the air was heavy with the smell of dog and we could hear them barking, there were no dogs to be seen. Also no people, no furniture and no light. The only light source in the room was the fading sunlight coming in through the window we'd just entered. I heard some human voices upstairs and some barking coming from downstairs and both sets of voices sounded vicious. I didn't like being here. I looked at

Mo. Her eyes glowed a little in the darkness.

"Where would he be?" She whispered.

"I don't know." I answered, "The animal activity seems to be coming from downstairs."

There was a stairway leading down directly across from our window. She nodded in that direction. Since we had smelled the scent of enraged pit bull since we had entered that house but hadn't seen one, it was safe to assume that the dogs were restrained. Regardless it was still a stupid idea to go down those stairs. But I went anyway and Molasses was close behind.

At the sixth step down I could see into the room into which we were descending. It was a pretty big unfinished basement with the floor and walls made of concrete. It suddenly got cold, as if the temperature had dropped twenty degrees. In the middle of the room was a crude ring with a diameter of about eight feet. It was surrounded by a three foot high wall. The room was empty except for a bunch of folding chairs stacked against a wall. "This must be where the magic's going to happen." I whispered as we reached the bottom of the stairway.

Molasses didn't respond. She was staring at the open doorway on the other side of the room. It was the source of the barking that we'd heard upstairs. I didn't hear or smell any humans in there. She looked at me. I nodded. We crept towards the doorway, keeping low and moving along the walls. When we got to the doorway we stopped and poked our heads into the next room. Molasses gasped at what we saw.

It was a much smaller room, longer but a lot more narrow than the room we were coming from and on one side of it was about a dozen cages built from two by fours and chicken wire. The cages were stacked on top of one another, so that there were three rows containing four cages. There was a pit bull inside each cage and none of them looked happy about their present situation. They looked hungry and mean with glowing red eyes glaring out from their hard, scarred faces.

There were a few more cages lined up against the wall at the far end of the room that we couldn't see from the doorway. We were going to have to fully enter the room to see if one of those cages contained Molasses's brother (or friend, or whatever). We'd come this far so there didn't seem to be any point in hesitating now. I walked into the room as casually as I could, looked up at the cages and said, "What's up, dogs?"

The room went insane. The dogs unleashed a torrent of mean, nasty barks and growls. They rammed themselves into the chicken wire but fortunately the cages were much sturdier than they looked. Ignoring the dogs, I walked past the first section of cages so that I could see into the next section. Molasses followed close behind me, anxious to get a look. These cages were empty.

Molasses breathed a sigh of relief. "I want to find him." She said, "But not in here."

I said, "Good, now that we know for sure that he's not in here, can we leave?"

She was looking up. "What's that?"

I saw that she was staring at a round hole in the wall. It was a foot wide and about eight feet off the ground. "I think it's a laundry chute."

"A what?"

"The humans put their dirty clothes in it and they drop down here, where the washer and dryer would be. Then they don't have to carry a heavy basket down the stairs."

"Really?" She kept looking at it.

"Look, Butterscotch is not in there." I said. I was getting very impatient. "Now let's go before something bad happens."

"The only way you're leaving here is in little bits and pieces." said the last voice in the world that I wanted to hear at that particular moment.

"Hi, Nails!" I said, "You're looking good!" I was lying. She looked as hideous as ever. She stood in the doorway with her two henchmen on either side. Nine was glaring at me with ferocity, I imagine that he was replaying our previous encounter in his head and thinking that he was about to get his revenge.

He was probably right. They were blocking the only way out of the room and I really didn't think that I was going to be able to fight the three of them. The best I could hope for was to keep them busy long enough for Molasses to escape. Whatever was about to happen, I probably wasn't going to leave this room.

I took a step towards them to make sure that I was between them and Molasses.

"Look guys, we don't want any trouble!" I said. Then I whispered to Molasses, "I'll try to keep them busy. You get ready to run!"

"Are you a complete idiot?" she hissed. "Just follow me!"

Quick as lightning she spun around and jumped up at the empty cages that were behind us. She bounced off of the cages and propelled herself right into the laundry chute hole. Nails and her henchdogs were taken aback by this for a couple of seconds but then Nails recovered nodded her head in my direction and snarled "Well, get him!"

It didn't seem like a good idea to wait for them so I spun around and made the same jumps that Molasses had made. As I made the first leap towards the cages, I could feel one of the dogs teeth snapping shut just millimeters away from my tail. But they couldn't reach me and I ended up sitting next to Molasses in the laundry chute hole. I smiled at her. "Hey, Beautiful!"

The hole that we had jumped into had a very small ledge that we were sitting in and then went back into a very steep diagonal aluminum surface for about half a foot and then it was a completely vertical shaft going up to the first floor. It was pretty much a big metal tube that was way too steep for even a cat to climb. Obviously people would drop their dirty clothes into the metal shaft and they would fall down the chute and land on the basement floor. Why they just didn't throw the clothes down the stairs was anybody's guess. It was a simple domestic convenience that was now saving me and Molasses's lives.

Nails walked up to the wall until she was directly beneath us. "You can't stay up there forever."

"Oh, I don't see why not." I answered. "It's not too snug of a fit and the company is certainly nice." I winked at Molasses who was looking a little nervous.

Nails on the other hand was suddenly looking very smug. That was not a good thing. "Hey Nine!" she called, "You busy?"

He trotted up to her. "Naw, Boss. What do you need?"

"How would you like to go upstairs and take a ride down the laundry chute?"

Nine's scarred face broke into a big smile. "After the way they made a fool out of me yesterday? I would love to."

"What's going to happen?" Molasses whispered.

"Nine is going to drop down the laundry chute." I replied. "When he hits the bottom of the chute, he'll knock us right into the waiting fangs and claws of Nails and Seven" I looked at Nails. "Is that the plan?"

"You got it." She snarled. "Nobody said that you weren't smart. Just not smart enough."

Nine laughed and said "I'll be right back!" He happily trotted out of the room.

It was a bad situation. All of the dogs in the cages were going nuts, barking and growling all kinds of rude things. Nails was waiting on the concrete floor directly beneath me, looking up at us and working her mouth in practice chomps, giving Molasses and me a preview of what she was going to do to us. Seven sat next to her, quiet but still menacing. It suddenly occurred to me that I had never heard Seven speak. Could he speak? Had he suffered some injury that had rendered him unable to utter a sound?

Then I realized that Molasses wasn't as nervous anymore. Sitting so close to her, I could tell that for some reason she had calmed slightly down. Given our current situation, that made no sense. Had she noticed something that could get us out of this mess? I certainly wasn't seeing anything in the room that would have a calming effect.

Was she hearing something comforting? I listened up. I had already been hearing the caged dogs barking insanely and the sound of Nine climbing the stairs. Was there anything else? Yes! I could hear car doors slamming outside. A bunch of cars and SUVs were now outside the house, I had been too preoccupied to hear them driving up and parking but Molasses must have heard them. Next I could hear at least eight men approaching the front of the house while three were going towards the back. There were also four dogs out there. For all I knew, these were more bad humans with dogs for the dogfights that were going to happen tonight. Whoever they were, I might be able to use the interruption to find some way to escape.

I was thinking about this when I heard somebody outside yell, "Open up! It's the police!"

That caused all kinds of frenzied activity in the humans on the second floor. Whatever they were doing didn't matter as a couple of seconds later the front and back doors were busted open and the cops and dogs stormed

87

into the house.

Taking a chance, I yelled, "Hey Duke! We're in the basement!"

I could hear dogs bolt for the basement and a man yelling, "Hey, Duke! Come back, boy!"

Nails and Seven also heard what was going on and they were not happy. Seven had turned to stare at the door to see who was about to come in while Nails just kept glaring at us with pure hate.

Four dogs burst into the room. Duke, Rowdy and two actual official K-9 corps dogs that I didn't know. The caged dogs took the barking up a notch but nobody cared. Nails had turned to face the doorway as she and Seven crouched into a fighting stance and emitted low, steady growls.

One of the K-9 corps dogs stepped forward and said, "Stand down, you two. You're under arrest."

I would've guessed that Nails would be the type of dog that would resist arrest and I would be correct. Nails jumped at the cop dog as soon as he had stepped into range. It didn't matter as Duke had pounced up and was on her before she could do any damage. He clamped his jaws around her neck, plucking her out of mid-air. Then he jerked his head and released his grip, flinging her into the nearest wall. She smashed hard into the cinderblock wall, slid to the floor and stayed there. Seven didn't move. He stayed in his fighting stance but he wasn't moving a muscle. I didn't know what had happened to Nine, but he obviously was no longer a threat. Molasses had fully relaxed and rubbed against me. Footsteps were coming down the stairway in the next room and the two cop dogs trotted off to meet their masters, leaving Duke and Rowdy to guard the prisoners. Rowdy was looking pretty shocked as he stared at the crazed dogs in the cages. Duke just maintained a professional attitude as he kept watch over Nails and Seven.

When he looked up at Molasses and me, I gave him a wink. "Hey Duke!" I said, "I think I might have some information about those dogfights you were talking about

the other day."

CHAPTER 8

Duke managed to sneak Molasses and me out of the
house, past the police and animal control officers that were
all over the place. All of the cops seemed pretty horrified
at what had been going on in that house. The human
criminals had all been arrested and taken away and I had
never even gotten a look at them. Nails, Seven, Nine and
all of the other dogs had been taken by animal control and
put in vans. Nails screamed on the way out about all of the
terrible things that she was going to do to me.

Duke led us out of the house and to the backyard where
we sat in the grass right behind the house. Night had
fallen, but there was still plenty of light from the big fat
moon overhead. If that wasn't enough, the trees were
showing the flashing red and blue lights pulsing from the

cop cars up front. Duke sat down in the grass, facing the back of the house. Molasses and I sat facing him, with our backs to the house. I was right next to the big wooden barrel that caught the runoff rain from the roof. I could sense that the barrel was full of water but I figured that none of it would spill on us.

I looked at Duke. "Excellent timing, Duke my man. How did you find us?"

"I got a tip!" He growled angrily.

That seemed odd. He should have been happy about getting a tip like that. He was probably a hero. Why would he be mad? There was only one reason I could think of. "From Yoshi?" I asked.

"Yes!" hissed a voice. I almost jumped out of my skin when Yoshi walked out from around the corner of the house.

I don't want to overstate how shocked and surprised I was to see Yoshi there but in the years that I had known him, he had only gone outside for trips to the vet and even then under extreme and violent protest. To see him out and about on Halloween night was the last thing that I would have ever expected to see. He looked fine, only someone who knew him as well as me could have seen how furious he was.

Duke's mood seemed to lighten. "I've known Yoshi since he was a kitten and I've never seen him as scared as when he came to tell me where you were."

That puzzled me. "How did he know where I was?"

Yoshi spoke up. "Well, it certainly wasn't from you, now was it? When a situation like this arises, you have been trained to report to me before you take any action!"

Duke snorted. "Like that would have done any good!" He looked at me. "Look kid, from what I saw in there you came real close to going to the big litter box in the sky. You knew that all you had to do was call me and I could've gotten the Sheriff to raid the place. Why would you do something so incredibly stupid as going in there by yourself?"

I didn't have anything to say. My mind was so occupied with trying to figure out how Yoshi could have known where I was that I couldn't come up with a good excuse.

Molasses decided to speak. "Don't be mad at Gatsby. He was just helping me."

Yoshi snorted. Duke laughed out loud and said, "Lady, I know why he went in there. I'm sure that if you asked him to jump into a shark tank to fetch your collar, he'd dive in and we'd all have fish for dinner. I was trying to make a point and the point is —"

"Maury!" I said. "You had Maury the mouse following Molasses! That's how you knew where we were!"

"No." said Yoshi.

"Aw, come on! He's pretty close." squeaked a voice from the darkness. Maury emerged from behind a tree.

"OK, then, who were you following?" I demanded.

Maury looked at Yoshi. Yoshi gave him a nod and Maury answered my question. "I was actually following Smokey."

Yoshi said, "Tell him."

"Yoshi asked me to shadow a cat named Smokey. I picked him up this afternoon after he talked to you guys."

This was weird. Usually this little rat was too intimidated by cats to say two words without stammering. Apparently whatever he had done tonight had filled him with confidence. I'd have to do something about that tomorrow but for now I just listened to his report.

"I tailed my quarry around the neighborhood for a few hours while he did nothing of particular significance."

"C'mon rat!" I said, "Move the story along."

He hesitated for a second, then licked his whiskers and continued, "My subject then met three pit bulldogs and engaged in conversation. I couldn't get close enough to hear what they were saying."

That surprised me. "Whoa! Smokey and those dogs met and had a talk?"

"Yeah, for about five minutes. They all seemed kind of mad. When the conversation broke up, I switched my surveillance to the pit bulls and followed them to this house. They entered the house and stayed inside. I was watching the house when I saw you and Molasses enter. At that point I ran back to report to Yoshi. Then he went out and found Duke."

Yoshi shot me a withering look. "Imagine that," he said. "He saw something potentially dangerous and reported to me."

Molasses turned to me and asked, "Who's Smokey?"

I turned to her and said, "He's a cat who told us that he got attacked by our three dog friends right after you and I first encountered them. He said that they beat him up as a message to me to keep away from you."

"Me? What the heck? I never saw them before that night!"

Yoshi said, "Do you know a cat named Smokey?"

"No."

He asked me to describe Smokey to her.

"Well," I said, "He's a little guy about nine pounds. His color is dark grey which is where I suppose he got his name. His biggest characteristic is his attitude. He's a complete jerk. Mean, nasty and he won't use any clean words if he can think of five or six dirty words that will do just as well. If you don't know him you're not missing a thing. He's just a sour little —"

"You talking about me?" Smokey emerged from around the corner of the house. Preston the German Shepherd was right beside him.

"Thanks for bringing him." Duke told Preston. "Did you have any trouble finding him?"

"Naw, he was in the vicinity just like Yoshi said he would be."

Duke turned to Yoshi. "Okay he's here. Now what?"

"Yeah, what do you want now?" Smokey demanded with all of his usual charm.

"Actually if you don't mind, could you move a little closer to Gatsby? I don't want to have to raise my voice."

Smokey seemed hesitant but Preston growled, "Move it!" and he complied. He walked up until he was a couple feet away from me. This put him close to the house and right in front of the rain barrel. I figured that real reason Yoshi asked him to get closer to me was so that Molasses could get a closer look at him and when I glanced at her I noticed that she did seem to be staring at Smokey very intently.

Smokey didn't even look in her direction. Instead he addressed Duke. "OK, you sent that idiot dog to drag me here. What do you want? I don't know anything about those dogs besides what I already told you!"

Duke growled, "You better watch your mouth! Those pit bulls are now locked up in an animal control facility. I had you brought here because my, um, friend Yoshi is investigating an unrelated matter and thinks that you might know something about it."

All eyes turned to Yoshi. He looked at all of us in turn, from Molasses and me, to Smokey and Preston, to Maury then to Duke and Rowdy. "As most of you know, Gatsby and I were engaged by Miss Molasses to find her brother

Butterscotch. So far our efforts have been unsuccessful. I was hoping that Smokey might be able to help us."

Smokey turned up his scowl as far as it could go. "I don't think so!"

Yoshi smiled. "That's ok. I didn't think that this would go the easy way." Then he suddenly shouted, "Now Preston!"

Preston sprung into action. Or at least his butt did as he whacked the rain barrel with his rear end and the barrel fell over. A torrent of water spilled out and drenched Smokey.

Usually any cat in those circumstances would screech and run for the hills. Not Smokey. He just sat there soaked looking at mad as a wet ca-, well he just looked really mad. Then there was something else weird about him. The water had washed out his fur so that he didn't seem charcoal grey anymore. Blackness seemed to be dripping off of him.

"Hey Smokey!" I said "I think your mascara is running."

Molasses said "Butterscotch?"

I could see it now. After having been drenched with the water, Smokey wasn't white, but enough of whatever he had used to disguise himself had come off so that he was now a really light dirty grey but you could tell that he should be white.

Yoshi spoke up. "I'm sorry, but I really couldn't think of a better way to make the truth known."

Smokey or rather Butterscotch just glared at him.

Duke sighed. "OK Yoshi, would you like to tell us how you knew that Smokey was the missing cat?"

Yoshi blinked a couple of times. "Seriously? You guys really didn't know? Gatsby, what was that case you turned down from the Bascom house?"

I replied, "Somebody had knocked over the Bascoms' barbecue grill and their dog Lightning was being blamed for –" I stopped as I realized what he was getting at.

Yoshi continued. "That's right. A white cat disappears, a neighborhood grill is knocked over, leaving a mess of ashes and then a grey cat suddenly shows up. And no one but me drew any kind of conclusion from that?" He slowly shook his head silently bemoaning the fact that he was so much smarter than everyone else.

"Yeah, yeah" Duke snarled. "Go on."

"Well that was the most obvious part. I can guess at everything else and Butterscotch can confirm or deny what he wishes."

Butterscotch just sat there glaring.

Yoshi continued. "My first guess is that Butterscotch ran away from home of his own accord, but he was still keeping tabs on Molasses. When he found out that she was coming to me for help, he must've hired the pit bulls to scare me off. When that didn't work he had them rough him up a little so that he could warn me off in person or get a closer look at me."

Butterscotch snorted.

"Do you have a correction?" Yoshi asked.

"Naw," Butterscotch snarled, "You're telling the story, jerk."

"Oh, that's excellent!" Yoshi said. "That's the attitude that made me suspect that there was something not genuine about you. You were overacting the rough, gruff street cat routine. I've known many stray cats and none were as rude, abrasive or foul-mouthed as you were acting."

He got no reaction from Smokey, so he continued. "Anyway I need to get home so let me just say that there's only one thing that isn't clear. I know you ran away from home and created a secret identity. I know that you hired those pit bulls in an effort to protect your secret identity, probably paying them with the meat that was missing from the Rogers' freezer. I don't know how you met those dogs in the first place, but who cares? What I don't know is your motive. Why did you runaway? Was it the pressure of competing in the cat shows? Was it the primordial thrill of being on your own and surviving on your natural instincts. Well, have you got anything to say for yourself?"

Smokey/Butterscotch stood up and turned to face

Molasses. He shook himself a couple of times then stood as tall as he could in an effort to restore some of his dignity. In the full blue glow of the moon he just looked like a dirty, washed out fleabag to me.

He looked at Molasses as if there were no one else there and said, "I did it for love. I did it for you, Mo. I figured that if I wasn't around to compete in the cat show, you could finally win!"

She just looked at him blankly for a few seconds while she digested his explanation. Then she asked, "Then why would you send those pit bulls after me and Gatsby?"

"They weren't going to hurt you; they were just supposed to scare you off. I didn't want to be found until you had won first prize."

I jumped in "So why did you get that beating? There had to be a less painful way to warn us off or get a better look at us."

He gave me a scornful look. "The beating was for real. I told Nails that her performance with you that night was horrible and she beat me up a little."

"You filed a false report with us!" Rowdy squealed. Nobody paid him any attention.

Molasses was ready to speak and she didn't look happy. "So let me make sure that I have this straight. You ran away and scared me and our people half to death because you love me?"

"Yes! And I always have! I know you think of me as just your friend, but-"

She didn't let him finish. "And you actually thought that I'd be happy? You idiot! I don't need you throwing any cat shows for me! I can beat you on my own!"

He answered, "Well, you haven't yet." He probably should've just not said anything.

"Shut Up!" Molasses said, "You're coming home with me right now!"

All of the gruffness and obnoxiousness had jumped right out of Butterscotch. He seemed embarrassed as he began to walk away. Molasses was right on his heels. She turned her head to give me a wink and said, "I'll see you around."

Smokey/Butterscotch also turned his head to give me a glare.

"What are you looking at?" Mo asked him. "Keep walking! You just wait we get home!"

We could hear her berating him long after they had disappeared into the woods.

Things had quieted down. While we were in back chatting, the cops had just about finished up and most of the cars had driven off, taking the flashing lights with them. The only light source now was the big blue moon floating above our heads.

Maury the mouse spoke up. "Well, I've got to go. I can't wait to tell the wife how I saved Gatsby's life!"

That surprised me "You saved my what?"

"Well, you know, if I hadn't told Yoshi where you were, you would have been, uh, well those pit bulls would have chewed you up!"

You mean like this?" I said as I pounced at him. I

purposely landed at least a foot away from him but he didn't notice and took off running in fright. I yelled to his back that he'd better not go around telling anybody that he saved my life.

Yoshi said, "It may hurt your pride but he's right, you know."

"Yeah," I replied, "Now you're going to start. I know you're going to lay into me for not reporting back about this house."

He smiled. "Not at all. The enemies that you made tonight should be enough to teach you a lesson."

"What are you talking about?"

"Well, Butterscotch is pretty mad. Much angrier at you than he is at me. And he's extremely clever. I'd advise staying away from him, although that won't be possible if you're going to keep seeing Molasses.

I scoffed, "I can handle anybody named Butterscotch."

"Sure but what about Nails and her two lackeys. They're sure to hold a huge grudge against you."

I laughed. "What about them? They're in jail!"

Yoshi's smile turned into a smirk. "Until they escape."

Duke, who had been watching our discussion with amusement, took offence at that remark. "Animals do not escape from Animal Control!"

Yoshi wasn't impressed. "Except for all of the ones who have. What about Cinnamon, that cat we caught poisoning the Richardson's dogs? He broke out of the County Animal Shelter. And you'll remember Hector and Jesse, those stray dogs who were terrorizing the mailman. Were they even locked up for a whole day before they'd escaped? That Animal Control building might as well install revolving doors!"

Duke and Preston were both looking very irritated with Yoshi's disrespect of the Animal Control prison.

Yoshi turned back to me. "Anyway, maybe having to constantly watch your back for these new enemies will teach you a lesson. It's inexcusable that on Halloween night I had to come outside to save your neck!"

"You can stop." I interrupted. I could hear some people hanging around the front of the house. "I really do appreciate you braving the horrible outdoors just to help me out. I just hope those Goth kids I just saw up front don't come back here and see you. They'd probably love to get their hands on a black cat tonight. Who knows what kind of weird Halloween rituals they would use you for and -" I stopped speaking as I had turned to face Yoshi and he was no longer where he had been sitting.

Duke looked at me. "He got up and started running as soon as you said the word Goth."

I grinned back at him "He was probably at home under the bed by the time I said 'rituals'".

Preston was usually too authoritarian to laugh at my nonsense, especially when Duke was around but this was too much. We both cracked up. Duke said, "You'd think that he would've realized that the people up front are just the last cops finishing up."

As if on cue we heard a voice calling from up front.

"Duke! C'mon boy! Where are you?" It was Deputy Bishop, Duke's owner.

Duke turned to Preston. "We gotta go." Then he looked at me. "Hey kid, you've had a rough night. Do you need a lift home?"

I shook my head. "Nope. I can walk. I'll see you guys later." I watched as Duke and Preston trotted up to the front of the house. After a couple of seconds, a car door slammed and the last SUV drove off leaving the house.

Everything was quiet. The best route home was to cut through the woods. I wasn't in a hurry as Yoshi was sure to be in a foul mood. I just walked through the trees at a slow, leisurely pace as the blue moon shone down on me and I thought about how soon would be too soon to go see Molasses again.

THE END

Robert J. Smith is the pen name for Gatsby the cat. Gatsby lives with a human family and his friend Yoshi. Gatsby has held positions as a food critic, actor, mattress tester, mouse chaser and is proud of ability to type without opposable thumbs.

YOSHI AND GATSBY RETURN IN:

PETECTIVES: CHRISTMAS PARTY

Christmastime is here! But someone not filled with the holiday spirit is trying to kill an obnoxious dog and cat detective Gatsby finds himself in the crossfire. If Gatsby survives, he wants to throw a Christmas Eve blowout for the neighborhood animals. His partner Yoshi is dead set against the party but he may be able to use it to unmask a would-be killer and teach Gatsby what Christmas is all about. Throw in a canine love triangle and a cute orphan and you've got the recipe for one riveting Yuletide affair. The Petectives are throwing a Christmas party and you don't want to miss it!

AN EXCERPT:
CHAPTER 1

It was late December and the sounds of jingle bells filled the air. The bells weren't coming from any horse drawn sleighs but from the stupid bell on the collar that the little girl that I lived with had put on me last night. The collar was a red and green striped nylon strap with a black plastic clasp and a brass bell on the front directly under my chin. I didn't mind the people putting a collar around my neck, but what was the point of the bell?

I found the ringing from the bell to be highly annoying as I walked along the suburban sidewalks on my way to an appointment. It was an extremely cold night that made me grateful that I'd been born with a thick, orange striped coat. A severe ice storm had hit earlier that day and everything looked like it was coated with thick, clear glass. It was as if the houses and trees were glazed donuts and it made everything outside look beautiful, especially the houses that had Christmas lights. The ice seemed to heighten the effect of the colorful lights, making them even brighter and cheerier against the dark winter night. Despite all of the beauty, the ice had caused some damage and every so often I had to walk around a fallen tree branch or even a downed tree. The power had gone out at my house for a couple of hours, but since my people had left town to visit relatives for the Christmas holiday, nobody had really been inconvenienced.

Actually the atmosphere inside my house had gotten pretty icy as well. Our people had gone to visit relatives and wouldn't be back until after Christmas. The house was just occupied by me and my housemate Yoshi, which gave me the idea that we should throw a big Christmas party for all of the neighborhood animals.

"Absolutely not." Yoshi had said when I'd presented the idea to him a couple of hours ago. "I won't have every filthy dog and cat in the area wreaking havoc on my house."

This seemed a little strident to me since I lived there too, but he was older which made him the alpha cat and therefore what he says goes. Or so he thought. "Oh, come on," I replied, "Every pet left behind by their family wants to throw a huge party. Let's live the dream."

"Let's not"

"C'mon, where's your Christmas spirit?"

At that point he rolled his eyes at me and said, "What do you know about Christmas spirit? What do you know about Christmas?"

"What don't I know? I've watched about fifty gazillion Christmas specials with the kids. I know everything about Christmas."

"I doubt that," he answered. "Christmas means a bit more than what you're likely to absorb from the pabulum fed to you from children's television. In any event we will not be having a party in this house. "

I kept trying and he kept denying and the end result was that when I left the house for my appointment, he and I were barely on speaking terms. Hopefully my meeting would lead to an interesting case which would ease some of the tension between the two of us.

My meeting was on the corner of Fillmore and Pershing, in front of a house with a lit-up seven foot tall inflated snowman. Classy. I was about a block away and I could see a cat standing in the snow about five feet in front of the decoration.

As I got closer, I got a better look at her. She was a bit older than me, but the years were treating her very well. She was a medium sized brown cat with black patches on her back and belly. Although her fur was heavier than mine, she looked like she was freezing.

"Penelope?" I called as I trotted across the lawn towards her. The footing was much better on the lawn than it had been on the iced over sidewalks.

She nodded. "Please call me Penny. You must be the cat who works for Yoshi."

"I work with Yoshi," I corrected her, "It's not like he pays me."

She raised her eye whiskers. "I didn't mean to offend you."

I smiled at her to show her that we were friends. "You didn't. Now what did you want to see me about?"

he hesitated for a second and then said, "I hate to say it, but I was kind of hoping that Yoshi would show up with you."

I laughed. "Lady, the only appointments Yoshi shows up for are mealtimes and naptimes. And he wouldn't show up for those if they were outside of our house."

"That doesn't sound like the Yoshi I used to know." She said doubtfully, as if she thought that I was lying. I might have taken offense at that, if I hadn't been so intrigued by the last four words of her sentence.

"You used to know Yoshi?" I asked. "When?"

"Oh, I used to live in this neighborhood." She said. "My girl went to college about five years ago and I went with her. She hasn't been able to find a job since she graduated so we moved back in with her parents a couple of weeks ago."

"Well, welcome back. So can I help you with something? Or did you just want to talk about old times with Yoshi?"

"No, I've got a problem. I think that someone is trying to kill my friend. About a week ago –". She stopped talking and gave me an odd look. I realized that I had a big grin on my face.

"Sorry," I said, "I'm not happy that someone's trying to kill your friend. It's just that my life's been kind of boring for the last couple of months. The prospect of stopping someone from doing away with someone else makes me a little enthusiastic."

She looked doubtful. "Doesn't that mean that you are in fact happy that someone's trying to kill my friend?"

I started to reply but before the words came out of my mouth she said, "Never mind. I suppose that it's good that you're enthusiastic about your work. Can I continue?"

I saw no point in saying anything so I nodded.

She continued. "About a week ago, Thor, the dog that I live with got sick. Violently ill. He would've died if our people hadn't gotten him to the vet in time."

"Sounds bad."

"It was, they had to pump his stomach."

"Is he okay?" I asked.

"He is now. He spent a couple of days at the animal hospital but he seems alright now."

"How did the poison get into him?"

"There was a piece of bologna on the ground in the backyard. He said that it smelled funny but he ate it

119

anyway. Apparently it had been soaked in some kind of liquid fertilizer."

She was interrupted when a harsh wind blew at us. When things had quieted down, I asked, "Why would he eat the bologna if it smelled funny?"

She shrugged. "It was a piece of bologna. He's on a special diet so he doesn't get to eat anything other than dry dog food. He jumps at any treat that he sees." Then she cocked her head and said, "Listen."

The wind had died down and the night was very still. All I could hear was a couple of dogs a couple of blocks away, loudly barking. One dog was much louder than the other. They seemed to be debating the merits of drinking water from a hose versus gulping it out of the toilet.

"Is he one of the dogs engaged in the philosophy discussion?" I asked.

"Yep. Loud, isn't he?"

"A little. You must get a lot of noise complaints – from Russia."

She smiled. "He can be loud and opinionated. Even obnoxious. But he's the most loyal friend you could ever have." The smile went away. "Somebody tried to hurt him. I want to know who."

"I think we can help you."

"Great!" she perked up again, "Come with me and I'll introduce you to Thor."

"Whoa, I can't tonight. I have a previous engagement. How about I drop by your house tomorrow morning around ten?"

"That would be great! Maybe Yoshi could come and – "

"I doubt that," I interrupted. "I don't know what he was like five years ago but like I said before, Yoshi is strictly an indoor cat. He wouldn't leave our house unless it was on fire and even then it would be under protest."

"He sounds so different. Maybe I'll come around sometime and see him."

"Sure, you do that. I'll see you tomorrow morning."

"That's fine." She smiled again. "I'll see you tomorrow." She winked at me and strolled off in the direction of the dog barking.

I watched her for a minute and then took off in the opposite direction.

CHAPTER 2

I was in a pretty good mood as I strolled off to my next appointment. We now had a client with an interesting case and the interview hadn't made me late for my date.

My good mood was somewhat broken when I got about five houses away from my destination and I didn't smell the girl I was going to meet. If she was where she was supposed to be, I would've caught her scent by now, even in this frosty air. Where was she? I didn't have to wonder for long. I could hear a big commotion from behind the houses I was walking past. Barking and hissing and spitting that was even loud enough to drown out the bell around my neck. The one doing all of the hissing was my date, the one and only Molasses. I took off and ran up the driveway that I happened to be in front of at full speed, or as full as I could get with all of the ice that covered all of the driveways and lawns. I headed back between two houses and when I got to the backyard I jumped very carefully onto an ice coated chain link fence and ran a few feet down it until I could get a good view of what was happening.

The full moon reflecting off of all the ice illuminated a grim scene. A chase was approaching me. It was about four backyards away and coming fast but I could clearly see two cats being chased by a vicious dog. I recognized two out of the three participants. The cat running in the lead was my girlfriend. She was a medium sized cat, white with black patches and cute as a button even while running for her life. Her name was Molasses and at this particular moment her name seemed ironic as she was moving faster than I'd ever seen a cat move. Running right next to her was a kitten that I didn't recognize. He had no collar and was orange, but not as orange and stripey as me. His tiny legs were pumping hard to keep up with Molasses.

The dog chasing them was someone I knew well. He was a bulldog named Percy who was usually chained to the railing on his back porch. As fast as he was running, I could still see the chain dangling from his neck trailing on the ground behind his grey muscled body. He had been threatening to break free for years and apparently it had finally happened. The most likely explanation for what was happening was that Percy had been going after the kitten, Molasses had come along and tried to defend the little guy and now Percy was trying to turn them both into chew toys.

I was pretty sure that the only thing that was going to distract Percy from his prey was more desirable prey. I certainly fit that description, having spent years mocking him from beyond the range of his chain. I knew that he would love to sink his teeth into me. There was only one thing to do.

I was still atop the chain link fence and I stood as best I could while making sure that I didn't slip on the icy surface. The procession was only a backyard away from me and approaching fast.

"Hey Percival!" I shouted. "What's up, dog?"

The chase instantly stopped. At least Percy did. Molasses and her friend kept running. The both of them kept going, vaulted the fence that I was standing on and hit the ground running on the other side. Percy had lost interest in them and was glaring at me.

"Gatsby! Oh, I'm going to enjoy this." He said in a tone that clearly implied that I wasn't going to be enjoying anything ever again.

"Merry Christmas!" I said in as cheery a voice I could manage.

"I guess that I was an extra good boy this year!" He growled, "Getting a hold of you has been on my Christmas list for years."

Molasses and company were long gone at this point. I was free to put my plan in action. The plan that I had hastily conceived in three seconds that probably wouldn't work. It occurred to me that it might be a better idea to try talking to him

"So, Percy," I began. That was actually all that I managed to get out as he picked that moment to attack.

He jumped five feet in the air right at me. There's no way he should've been able to jump that high but I guess that shows how much he hated me. As soon as I saw him tense up to jump at me, I leapt off of the fence, hitting the ice covered ground running. I headed back the way I had come, even stepping in the same footprints I had made when I had been running towards the fence. Percy was hot on my heels which was weird. There was no way a bulldog should have been as fast as me but he was right on my tail and would probably catch me in a second or two. The best guess was that his legs were being powered by all the years of frustration that my taunts from just beyond the range of his chain had caused.

In an instant we had covered the thirty feet from the fence that I'd been sitting on to the house's driveway. As soon as I got to the edge of the driveway, I leapt straight up into the air and executed a perfectly timed back flip. Percy ran right beneath me. When he realized that I was no longer in front of him, he tried to spin around to get back after me. Sadly for him spinning around on a driveway coated with about a half inch of ice wasn't easy. As soon as he tried to turn, he lost his footing and began to slip. I watched his face as it went from an expression of horrible anger to absolute horror.

I had complained earlier that it was a steep climb to get to the backyard of that house but now it was a pleasure to see Percy slipping and sliding down that slickened driveway. After he'd gone about three feet, he collapsed, fell on his belly and started spinning around with his paws outstretched. He went down the driveway until I couldn't see him and I assume that from there he slid out into the street and wouldn't stop until he hit the curb on the opposite side. But he heard me exclaim as he slid out of sight, "Merry Christmas, Fool! And to all a good night!"

I realize that that may have been a bit much, but what the hey, it's Christmas.

CHAPTER 3

I caught up with Molasses about three blocks away. She and her kitten friend were walking across the lawns of another residential street.

"Hey, what was that all about?" I asked as I approached them.

Molasses glanced down at her companion and then answered, "All I know is that Percy got loose and was chasing this little guy."

At close quarters the little guy looked a little different. He was orange like me but he had a white shock of fur on his chest and matched the white on all four of his paws. I would have guessed him to be about four months old. He was certainly skinny, even for a kitten. I wondered when was the last time he'd eaten. "Hey little guy. What's your name?"

"Nothing." He said quietly as he stared at the ground.

"Nothing?" I asked Molasses.

"He doesn't seem to have a name." She said.

"Not much of a talker, is he?"

"That's ok," she said as she gave him a reassuring smile. "I like my men strong and silent."

That should have gotten a smile out him. Or an embarrassed grimace. Or at the very least, a shrug. He had no reaction whatsoever; he just kept looking at the ground.

Molasses continued, "Percy must have finally broken loose from his chain and was chasing this cute little guy. I tried to help and you saw the result of that."

"Cute?" I repeated. I looked at the kitten. "Hey dude, are you trying to steal my girlfriend?"

I was just messing with him to see if I could get a reaction. He just kept studying the frosted grass between his paws.

Molasses broke the silence. "Don't be silly," she said, "We need to get him off of the streets. He's been roaming around by himself for the last few days."

"In this weather?" I said incredulously, "He must be a tough little nut."

That got a reaction out of the kitten. The corners of his mouth went up in what I took to be a quick flash of a grin. If I had blinked I would have missed it but he definitely smiled.

Just then we were given a harsh reminder of exactly where we were and what time of the year it was. A savage wind that must have originated in the Arctic and travelled down through Alaska and Canada blasted right through us.

"Whoa," I exclaimed after the wind had died down, "This is not weather for cats to be out and about in. Where can we drop this kid off so we can go back to my house?"

Molasses just looked at me.

"You want to take him with us?"

She smiled her special smile at me. This had the effect of making me feel much warmer. "Well," she said, "I was hoping that maybe he could stay with you for a couple of days."

I was aghast. "What! Are you kidding?"

"Oh, why not? Your people are out of town until after Christmas. It's just you and Yoshi in that big house."

"Oh!" I exclaimed. "What's Yoshi going to say if I bring home some strange kitten that I hardly know? He'll freak out!"

"I'd take him to my house but my people are there and you know that Butterscotch would be mean to him!"

Butterscotch was the sour little cat that lived with Molasses. He didn't like most other creatures in general and me in specific. I imagined that he would not like this kitten at all. I had begun to change my mind about bringing him to my house. With the way that Yoshi and I had been fighting, there was no telling how he would react if I brought home a stray kitten. There was the potential for some hilarity.

"OK." I said, "He's coming home with me."

END OF EXCERPT – Read the rest of the story by picking up PETECTIVES: CHRISTMAS PARTY by Robert J. Smith

Made in the USA
Middletown, DE
12 February 2017